Who's at the Door?

Jonathan Allen

Tambourine Books  New York

Library of Congress Cataloging in Publication Data

Allen, Jonathan. Who's at the door?/by Jonathen Allen.—1st U.S. ed. p cm.
Summary: Determined to have the three little pigs for dinner,
the wolf tries all sorts of disguises to get into their house.
[1. Wolves—Fiction. 2. Pigs—Fiction. 3. Humorous stories.] I. Title.
PZ7.A427246Wh 1993 [E]—dc20 92-19618 CIP AC
ISBN 0-888-12257-4
1 3 5 7 9 10 8 6 4 2
First U.S. edition, 1993

The three little pigs lived in a small house in the woods. The big bad wolf also lived in the woods. He desperately wanted to eat the little pigs for dinner. But to do this, he had to get inside their house. It was a tough problem.

Not long afterward there was a third knock at the door. The three little pigs peered through the window but they could not see anyone.

1 don't think there's anyone there.

But 1 heard a knock.

Let's open the door and see who it is.

While the pigs were busy plotting,
they heard the front door opening.
But they were prepared.

A very large and hairy pig was standing inside the door.
Hello? Anyone at home? It's your long lost cousin, Harry Maurice.
Can I come in? The door seems to be open.

No sooner had Harry come in and shut the door behind him than there was a loud knocking noise.

Ooh!
There's someone at the door.

I'd better open it and see what he wants.

There, standing on the doorstep, was a great big wolf with long, sharp teeth and a mean expression on his face.

I'm the very big, very bad wolf, and I've come to eat you up, piggy!

I'm not really a piggy. I'm a wolf just like you!

Well, you look like a piggy. Prepare to be eaten.

You'll have to catch me first.

The three clever little pigs held a party to celebrate.